More Shakespeare & STORIES

Retold by

**ANDREW MATTHEWS
& TONY ROSS**

ORCHARD

ORCHARD BOOKS

This text was first published in Great Britain in the form of a gift collection called
The Orchard Book of Shakespeare Stories, illustrated by Angela Barrett in 2001
This first edition of each story first published in paperback in 2003 by Orchard Books
This bind-up edition published in 2014
This edition published in 2018 by The Watts Publishing Group

3 5 7 9 10 8 6 4 2

Text copyright © Andrew Matthews, 2001
Illustrations copyright © Tony Ross, 2002

The moral rights of the author and illustrator have been asserted.

A CIP catalogue record for this book
is available from the British Library.

ISBN 978 1 40833 384 6

Printed and bound by CPI Group (UK) Ltd, Croydon, CR0 4YY

The paper and board used in this book are from
well-managed forests and other responsible sources.

Orchard Books
An imprint of
Hachette Children's Group
Part of The Watts Publishing Group Limited
Carmelite House
50 Victoria Embankment
London EC4Y 0DZ

An Hachette UK Company
www.hachette.co.uk

www.hachettechildrens.co.uk

Contents

A Midsummer Night's Dream   5

     Cast list   6

     A Midsummer Night's Dream   8

     Love and Magic   62

The Tempest   65

     Cast list   66

     The Tempest   69

     Power in the Tempest   122

Hamlet 125

Cast list 126

Hamlet 129

Revenge in Hamlet 182

Henry the Fifth 185

Cast list 186

Henry the Fifth 189

Patriotism in Henry the Fifth 242

A Midsummer Night's Dream

Cast List

Hermia

In love with Lysander

Helena

Friend to Hermia
In love with Demetrius

Demetrius

Betrothed to Hermia

Lysander

In love with Hermia

Oberon

King of the Fairies

Titania

Queen of the Fairies

Puck

An Elf

Bottom

A Weaver

The Scene

In and around Athens, Ancient Greece.

Ay me, for aught that I could ever read,
Could ever hear by tale or history,
The course of true love never did run smooth,

Lysander; I.i.

A Midsummer Night's Dream

When the path of true love runs smoothly,
the world seems a wonderful place – all
bright skies and smiling faces.

Unfortunately, true love has a habit of
wandering off the path and getting lost,
and when that happens people's lives get
lost too, in a tangle of misery.

Take the love
of Duke Theseus
of Athens and
Hippolyta, Queen
of the Amazons, for
instance. They were to
be married, and their happiness spread
through the whole of Athens. People had
decorated their houses with flowers, and
left lamps burning in their windows at
night, so that the streets twinkled like a
city of stars. Everybody
was joyful and excited
as they prepared to
celebrate the Duke's
wedding day.
Well, almost
everybody…

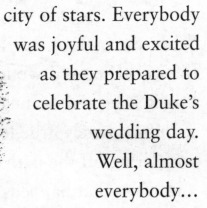

On the day before the royal wedding, two friends met by chance in the market square: golden-haired Hermia, and black-haired Helena, both beautiful and both with secrets that made their hearts ache.

For a while, the two friends chatted about nothing in particular. Then Helena noticed a look in Hermia's deep blue eyes that made her ask, "Is everything all right, Hermia?"

Hermia looked so sad and serious.

"I am to marry Demetrius tomorrow," she replied.

"Demetrius!" said Helena softly. Now her heart was aching worse than ever. Night after night she had cried herself to sleep, whispering Demetrius's name, knowing that her love for him was hopeless.

Many years ago the families of Hermia and Demetrius had agreed that, when they were of age, their daughter and son should marry. "You must be the happiest young woman in Athens!" sighed Helena.

"I've never been so miserable in my life!" Hermia declared. "You see, I don't love Demetrius."

"You don't?" cried Helena, amazed.

"I'm in love with Lysander," Hermia confessed, and she began to describe all the things that made Lysander so wonderful.

Helena thought about Lysander, with his curly brown hair and broad smile. He was *quite* handsome, she supposed, but he didn't have Demetrius's dark, brooding good looks. Why on earth did Hermia find him so attractive?

"Of course, I told my father that I didn't wish to marry Demetrius," Hermia said, "and he went straight to him to explain – but you know how stubborn Demetrius can be. He lost his temper and said it didn't matter who I loved, our marriage had been arranged and it must go ahead, no matter what. His stupid pride's been hurt, that's all – he doesn't love me a bit."

"Then who does he love?" Helena enquired eagerly.

"No one, except for himself," said Hermia. "I *can't* marry someone I don't love, and I know it will cause a scandal, but Lysander and I are going to run away together!"

"*When?*" Helena asked.

"Tonight," Hermia told her. "I'm meeting him at midnight in the wood outside the city walls. We plan to travel through the night, and in the morning we'll find a little temple where we can be married. Oh, Helena, it will be so *romantic*! Please say that you're happy for me!"

"Of course I am," said Helena. "I'm overjoyed."

And she was overjoyed – for herself. 'At last, this is my chance!' she thought.

'If I visit Demetrius tonight and tell him that Hermia and Lysander have gone off together, he'll forget about his pride…and then…when I tell him how I feel about him, he'll be so flattered, he'll fall in love with me. Love always finds a way!'

Which is true, but love doesn't always find the way that people expect, as Helena was about to find out. For it was not only in the human world that love was causing unhappiness; although Helena and Hermia did not know it, two different worlds would meet in the wood outside Athens that night, and the result would be chaos.

* * *

Oberon, King of
the Fairies, was
a creature of
darkness and
shadows, while his
wife, Queen Titania,
was moonlight and
silver. The two loved each

other dearly, but they had quarrelled
bitterly. Titania had taken
a little orphan boy as a
page, and made such
a fuss of the lad
that Oberon
had become
very jealous.
He wanted
the page
for himself.

That midsummer's night, in a clearing in the wood, Titania was singing to her page, while fairy servants fluttered around her like glittering moths.

When Oberon appeared, Titania's silvery eyes darkened. "Fairies, let us leave this place at once!" she said haughtily.

"Wait, Titania!" snapped Oberon.
"This quarrel of ours has gone on long
enough. You say I have no reason to be
jealous of the boy – very well, prove it!
Give him to me!"

"Not for all your fairy kingdom!"
hissed Titania. She raised her left hand,
and sent a ball of blue fire roaring across
the glade, straight at Oberon's head.

Oberon spoke a word of magic, and the fire turned to water that burst over him, drenching his clothes. By the time he had rubbed the water from his eyes, the glade was empty and Oberon was alone. "I'll make you sorry for this, Titania!" he vowed. Then, lifting his dripping head, he called out, "Puck? Come to me, now!"

A breeze sighed in
the branches, as an
elf dropped out of
the air and landed
at Oberon's feet.
The elf was
dressed in leaves
that had been sewn
together. His hair was
tangled, his skin as brown
as chestnuts, and when he smiled,
his white teeth flashed mischievously.
"Command me, master!" Puck said.

"I mean to teach the Queen a lesson,"
said Oberon. "Go, search the Earth and
fetch me the flower called Love in
Idleness."

"I will fly faster than a falling star!"
said Puck, and with that he had vanished.

A cruel smile played on Oberon's lips. "When Titania is asleep, I will drop the juice of the flower in her eyes," he said to himself. "Its magic will make her fall in love with the first living thing she sees when she wakes – perhaps a toad, or even a spider! She will make herself seem so ridiculous, that she will beg me to break the spell, and I will...after she's given me the page!"

This plan pleased Oberon so much that he began to laugh – but his laugh was cut short when he heard human voices approaching. With a wave of his fingers, Oberon made himself vanish among the shadows.

Demetrius, out searching for Hermia, halted in the middle of the glade, while he considered which path to take. This gave Helena a chance to catch up with him. "Wait for me, Demetrius!" she pleaded.

Demetrius scowled at her. "For the last time, Helena, go home!" he shouted angrily. "I can find Lysander and Hermia without your help."

"But you don't understand!" Helena exclaimed. "I love you! I've always loved you!"

She tried to put her arms around Demetrius, but he ducked away. "Well I don't love you!" he said roughly. "So go away and leave me alone!"

And he ran off through the moonlight.

"Oh, Demetrius!" sobbed Helena, running after him. "I would follow you through fire, just to be near you!"

✳ ✳ ✳

When the glade was once more still and silent, Oberon came out of the darkness. His face was thoughtful. "I must help that lovely maiden!" he whispered. "I know how cruel it is to love someone whose heart is so cold."

A wind brushed the Fairy King's cheek, and there stood Puck, holding a sprig of glimmering white flowers.

"Take two blossoms and search the woods for a young human couple," Oberon said to him. "Squeeze the juice of the petals into the young man's eyes, but do it when you are sure that the maiden will be the first thing he sees."

"At once, master!" Puck said with a bow, and then he was gone.

Then Oberon went to find Titania.
He found her sleeping alone on a bank of
violets, and the air was heavy with their
sweet perfume. As he dropped juice from
the magic flowers on to Titania's eyelids,
Oberon murmured:

> *"What you see when you awake,*
> *Do it for your true love take!"*

* * *

At that very moment, in another part of
the wood, Puck was putting magic juice
into the eyes of a young man he had
found sleeping next to a young woman at
the foot of a pine tree.

"When he wakes and sees her, his love
for her will drive him mad!" Puck giggled,
and he leapt into the air, like a grasshopper
in a summer meadow.

But, as bad luck would have it, Puck had found the wrong couple. Those sleeping under the tree were Lysander and Hermia, who had got lost in the wood and exhausted themselves trying to find the way out.

And as bad luck would also have it, a few seconds after Puck had left them, Helena wandered by, searching for Demetrius. Blinded by tears, Helena did not notice Lysander and Hermia until she stumbled over Lysander's legs.

He woke, saw her, and his eyes bulged like a frog's as the magic went to work.

"Lysander?" gasped Helena. "What are you doing here? I mean, you mustn't be here! Get away quickly! Demetrius is looking for you, and if he finds you..." Her voice trailed off – there was a strange look about Lysander, and it made her feel uncomfortable. "Why are you staring at me like that?" she asked.

"Because at last I have found my own true love," said Lysander. "Helena, can't you see how much I love you?"

Helena stepped back, laughing nervously. "Don't be silly, Lysander!" she said. "You love Hermia...don't you?"

"Hermia, who is she?" scoffed Lysander, scrambling to his feet. "How could I love anyone but you, with your eyes like stars, your hair as black as ravens' wings, and your skin as soft as...?"

"That's quite enough of that!" said
Helena. "This is some sort of midsummer
madness!"

"Madness? Yes, I'm mad!" said
Lysander. "Mad with love for you!
Come to my arms, and cool the fires
of my passion with your kisses!"

He moved towards Helena, but she
turned and fled. Lysander followed her,
shouting, "There's no escape from love,
Helena! This was meant to be!"

Their loud voices and pounding footsteps woke Hermia. "Lysander, where are you?" she muttered sleepily. "Don't wander off on your own, my love. You might be eaten by a lion, or a bear..." The very thought made her wide awake, and she sat up. "Or I might be eaten, come to that!" she said with a shudder. "I'm coming to find you, Lysander, so we can be eaten together!"

* * *

Not five paces from the bank of
violets where Titania lay asleep, a group
of Athenians had gathered in secret to
rehearse a play that they meant to perform
for Duke Theseus after his wedding. One
of the actors, a weaver called Bottom, was
behind a tree, waiting to appear
when he heard his cue.
"I'll show them how
it's done!" Bottom
said to himself.
"When the Duke
sees what a fine
actor I am, he'll
give me a purse
of gold, or my
name's not
Nick Bottom!"

He glanced up,
and saw a strange
orange light
circling the tree.
"Now what's
that, I wonder?"
he muttered.
"A firefly
perhaps?"

It was Puck.
He had noticed
the actors as he
flew by on his
way back to
Oberon, and had seen
a chance to make mischief.
"Behold, the Queen's new love!" he said.
Magic sparks showered down from his
fingertips on to the weaver.

Immediately Bottom's face began to sprout hair, and his nose and ears grew longer and longer. His body was unchanged, so Bottom had no idea that anything was wrong, until he heard his cue and stepped out from behind a tree.

Bottom had meant his entrance to be dramatic, and it certainly was. The other actors took one look at the donkey-headed monster coming towards them, and raced away screaming and shouting.

"What's the matter with them?" said Bottom, scratching his chin. "My word, my beard has grown quickly today! I'll need a good shave before the performance tomorrow!" He paced this way and that, puzzling out why his friends had left in such a hurry. "O-o-h! I see-haw, hee-haw!" he said at last. "They're trying to frighten me by leaving me alone in the wood in the dark! Well it won't work! It takes more than that to frighten a man like me-haw, hee-haw!"

And to prove how brave he was, Bottom began to sing. His voice was part human, part donkey and it sounded like the squealing of rusty hinges. It woke Queen Titania from her sleep on the bank of violets. "Do I hear an angel singing?" she said, and raised herself on one elbow and gazed at Bottom. "Adorable human, I have fallen wildly in love with you!" she told him.

"Really?" said Bottom, not the least alarmed by the sudden appearance of the Fairy Queen. He was sure it was all part of the trick his friends were playing.

"Sit beside me, so I can stroke your long, silky ears!" Titania purred. "My servants will bring you anything you desire."

"I wouldn't say no to some supper," said Bottom. "Nothing fancy – a bale of hay or a bag of oats would suit me fine!"

From up above came the sound of Puck's laughter, like the pealing of tiny bells.

Oberon's laughter set every owl in the wood hooting. "My proud Queen, in love with a donkey?" he cried. "Well done, Puck! Titania will think twice before she defies me again! But what of the humans?"

"I did as you commanded, master," said Puck. "I found them..."

A voice made him turn his head, and he saw Demetrius stamping along the path, dragging Hermia by the arm.

"That is the fellow!" said Oberon. "But who is that with him?"

"He is not the one I cast the spell on!" Puck yelped.

"Quickly," said Oberon. "Make yourself invisible before they see us!"

✳ ✳ ✳

Hermia was thoroughly miserable. Everything had gone wrong: she had found Demetrius instead of Lysander, and Demetrius was in such a foul temper that she feared the worst. "Oh, where is Lysander?" she wailed. "You've killed him, haven't you, you brute?"

With a weary groan, Demetrius let Hermia go and slumped to the ground. "I haven't touched your precious Lysander!" he yawned. "Now stop whining and get some sleep. When it's light, we'll find our way out of this accursed wood."

"I won't rest until I find Lysander!" Hermia said defiantly.

"Just as you wish," said Demetrius. "I'm too tired to argue any more."

He lay back among the ferns and closed his eyes. He heard Hermia walking away, and then he fell into a deep sleep.

Moonlight shifted and shivered as Oberon and Puck reappeared. "This is the man," said Oberon, peering down at Demetrius. "Search the wood for a black-haired maiden, and bring her here. When she is close by I will put magic juice in his eyes and wake him."

"Yes, master! But tell me, is human love always so complicated?" Puck asked curiously.

"Just do as I have commanded!" snapped Oberon.

✳ ✳ ✳

Helena was still running, with Lysander just a few steps behind her. So many bewildering things had happened to her, that when an orange light appeared above the path in front of her, she was not surprised – in fact, a curious idea suddenly popped into her mind – Puck's magic had put it there. Helena became convinced that if she followed the light, it would lead her

back to Athens, and sanity. Over streams and through clearings the light led her, until at last she came to a deep thicket of ferns, where she paused for breath.

"Helena, marry me!" she heard Lysander shout.

"I don't want you!" she shouted back. "I want Demetrius!"

"And here I
am, my love!"
said Demetrius,
springing up out
of the ferns nearby, his
eyes glowing with magic.
"Hold me, let me melt in your sweetness!"
Helena did not bother to wonder why
Demetrius had changed his mind: her
dreams had come true, and she was about
to rush into his arms
when Lysander ran
between them.

"Keep away
from her,
Demetrius!"
Lysander
said hotly.
"Helena is mine!"

"Lysander...is that you?" called a voice, and Hermia came stumbling out of the bushes. Brambles had torn the hem of her dress, and there were leaves and twigs stuck in her hair. "Thank the gods you're safe!" she said, weeping for joy. "Why did you leave me, my only love?"

"Because I can't bear the sight of you!" said Lysander. "I want to marry Helena."

"So do I!" Demetrius exclaimed. "And since she can't marry both of us, we'll have to settle the matter, man to man!"

He pushed Lysander's chest, knocking him backwards, then Lysander pushed Demetrius.

Hermia stared at Helena, her eyes blazing. "You witch! You've stolen my Lysander!" she screeched.

"I haven't stolen anybody!" Helena replied angrily. "This is all some cruel trick, isn't it? The three of you plotted together to make a fool of me – and I thought you were my friend!"

"Our friendship ended when you took Lysander away from me!" snarled Hermia.

And there might have been a serious fight, if Oberon had not cast a sleeping spell on all four of them. They dropped to the ground like ripe apples, Hermia falling close to Lysander and Helena collapsing at Demetrius's side.

Oberon and
Puck appeared
magically
beside them.
"Smear their eyes
with fairy juice!"
said Oberon. "This knot
of lovers will unravel when they wake."

As Puck hurried about his task, the air
was filled with the singing of fairy voices.
"The Queen!" Puck muttered in alarm.
"The Queen is coming!"

✳ ✳ ✳

Titania did not notice Puck and Oberon, or
the sleeping lovers. She could see nothing
but Bottom, whose jaws were stretched
open in a wide yawn. "Are you weary,
dearest one?" she asked him tenderly. "Rest
with me on these soft ferns."

"I feel a powerful sleep coming over me-haw, hee-haw!" said Bottom.

"Fairies, leave us!" ordered Titania.

The fairies flew away, leaving bright trails in the air. Titania cradled Bottom's head in her lap, and they both dozed.

Oberon and Puck crept close. Puck began to grin, but he stopped when he saw the sorrow in his master's eyes.

"There is no laughter in this!" Oberon sighed. "How I long for Titania to smile at me, as she smiled at this creature, and to feel her soft arms around me as I sleep! Break the spell on the human, Puck, while I deal with the Queen."

Oberon moved his hands, weaving shadows into magic as he chanted:

"Be the way you used to be,
See the way you used to see,
Wake, my Queen, and come to me!"

Titania opened her eyes, and when she saw Oberon she flew into his arms. "I am so glad that you are here, my love!" she said. "I had the strangest dream! I dreamed that I had fallen in love with a..."

"We will never quarrel again," Oberon promised. "Keep your page – have fifty pages if you wish! What does it matter, as long as we are together?"

Puck saw that the sky was getting lighter. "It's almost dawn, master!" he warned.

"Then we must leave!" said Oberon, and he, Titania and Puck faded into the pale morning light.

* * *

When the sun rose, its light woke Demetrius and Helena, who fell in love at first sight, then Lysander and Hermia, who fell in love all over again. There was much smiling, sighing and kissing, and soon Demetrius said, "Today is Duke Theseus's wedding day, as well as mine and Helena's. Come, my friends, the priest can marry us all at the same ceremony!"

And the lovers hurried off towards
Athens, laughing every step of the way,
the paths of their true love running
smoothly at last.

* * *

And as for Bottom, he woke some time later and clambered stiffly to his feet. "I thought I was...!" He mumbled. "I thought I had...!" Anxiously, he felt his face and ears, and then sighed with relief.

"What a midsummer night's dream!" he exclaimed. "I'll write a poem about it, and read it to Duke Theseus and his bride, and the Duke will say: 'Well done, noble Bottom! Here's some gold for you!'"

And he stumbled away through the ferns, making up lines of poetry and reciting them out loud as he went.

The eye of man hath not heard, the ear of man hath not seen, man's hand is not able to taste, his tongue to conceive, nor his heart to report what my dream was.

Bottom; IV.i.

Love and Magic in
A Midsummer Night's Dream

In *A Midsummer Night's Dream* Shakespeare brings together two worlds: the human world of Athens, and the fairy world of the woods outside the city. One world is ruled by law, the other by magic, and in both worlds trouble is brewing.

In the woods outside Athens, Oberon and Titania are busy arguing over a page boy. Meanwhile Demetrius, who is as stubborn as Oberon, is insisting on marrying Hermia, even though she loves someone else. Add a group of bickering actors, and Puck, a mischievous sprite, and madness follows.

The humans are made to love the wrong partners, and Titania falls in love with one of the actors, who has the head of a donkey!

When the human lovers begin to fight one another, the play comes close to tragedy, but magic sets things right. The humans find their true loves and Oberon realises that his love for Titania is stronger than his pride.

The Elizabethans believed in a 'midsummer madness' that was caused by the heat of the summer sun, and many of the characters in *A Midsummer Night's Dream* behave as if they have been touched by this madness.

The fairy world and the human world are thrown into chaos by love, and Shakespeare pokes fun at how lovers behave. And in the character of Bottom he makes fun of actors – and even playwrights like himself too!

The Tempest

Cast List

Miranda

Daughter to Prospero

Prospero

A wizard
The rightful Duke of Milan

Ariel

An airy spirit

Caliban

Servant to Prospero

Antonio

Duke of Milan
Brother to Prospero

Alonso

King of Naples

Prince Ferdinand
Son to the King of Naples

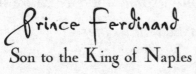

**Trinculo and
Stephano**
Sailors

The Scene

Mediterranean island in the fifteenth century.

O, I have suffered
With those that I saw suffer! A brave vessel,
Who had, no doubt, some noble creature in her,
Dashed all to pieces!

Miranda; I.iii.

The Tempest

A violent storm was raging over the
island. Palm trees bent and swayed like
dancers in the howling gale that tore off
their branches and sent them tumbling
through the air.

On a beach not far from the mouth of his cave, stood Prospero the wizard, his white hair and beard streaming out in the wind, his black robes flapping around him. As he

raised his left hand, thunder rumbled; he
lifted the staff in his right hand, and forked
lightning crackled, flickering like snakes'
tongues across the inky clouds.

Out to sea,
a ship with
broken masts
and tattered
sails wallowed
helplessly as the
storm drove it
towards a jagged coral-reef.

A lovely young woman in a white gown
hurried out of the cave
and ran towards
Prospero, her
dark hair
whipping about
her face. She
caught the
wizard by the
sleeve and called
out, "Father!"

Prospero seemed not to hear her. His eyes burned silver with magic, and they stayed firmly fixed on the ship.

"Father!" shouted the young woman. "What are you doing? Everyone aboard that ship will be killed!"

Above the sound of the wind came a groaning crash of timber striking rock. A huge wave reared up like a startled horse and thundered down on the ship, making it vanish from sight.

Prospero lowered his hands. The wind dropped to a gentle breeze, the boiling clouds faded into a blue sky and the sun glinted on a calm sea.

"No one has been harmed, Miranda," said Prospero. "Everything is as I planned. For your sake, I have used my magic to help right a great wrong, done long ago."

"What wrong, Father?" Miranda asked with a puzzled frown.

"Enough!" said Prospero. He moved
his left hand in front of Miranda's face,
and she fell into an enchanted sleep where
she stood.

Prospero took two paces towards the sea,
looking out at the place where the ship had
sunk. "Soon, my brother!" he whispered.

A sound made him turn his head in time to see a strange creature creeping up behind Miranda. It was shaped like a man, but its skin was covered with glistening green scales, and its eyes were as yellow as a lizard's.

"Caliban!"
Prospero said
sternly. "You
brought no
wood or water
to the cave this
morning. Must
I send the spirits
to torment you
again?"

Caliban scowled.
"I was not born to be
your servant!" he answered defiantly.
"My mother, the great witch Sycorax,
promised me that I would rule this
island, and so I would have – if you
had not come here, and stolen her books
of magic, and freed her slave-spirits to
help you drive her away!"

"Silence!" said Prospero, and he snapped his fingers.

Needles of fire seemed to lance through Caliban, forcing him to his knees. "Mercy, master, mercy!" he cried, bowing his head. The pain left him, and he hid his face so that Prospero could not see his cunning smile. "Why are you so cruel?" he whimpered. "You were kind to me once!"

"And you repaid my kindness by trying to kidnap my daughter!" snapped Prospero. "Get to work, you treacherous wretch!"

Caliban stood, and shambled off. "I will be revenged, one day!" he muttered to himself. "I will be King of this island, and I will take Miranda as my Queen!"

When Caliban was safely out of sight, Prospero lifted his staff. "Ariel!" he called softly. "Appear to me now, sweet spirit!"

There was a faint sound of music. Lights sparkled in the air, winking like sunshine on bursting bubbles. In the midst of the lights fluttered a young boy, with golden skin and white wings on his heels. He smiled at Prospero, and darted playfully around his head.

Prospero laughed. "Faithful Ariel!" he
said. "Are the sailors scattered over the
island as I commanded?"

"They are, good master," said Ariel, his
voice like the gentle humming of a harp.

"And where is Ferdinand, the King of
Naples' son?" Prospero demanded.

"Close by," said Ariel. "He mourns
his father, believing him to be drowned."

"He is not drowned," said Prospero. "He wanders the island lost, with my brother Antonio."  Prospero sighed, and old memories gave his face a far off look. "Twelve years ago, when I was Duke of Milan, my wife died," he said sadly. "Grief blinded me to the treachery of Antonio, who plotted in secret with my old enemy, King Alonso of Naples. They overthrew me, and Antonio took my place.

I was put in an open boat with my daughter, and cast adrift to die. But destiny took me to this island, to  Sycorax's magic books, and you. My spells brought the ship here, and now it is time for mischief and magic."

"And revenge, master?" said Ariel.

Prospero shook his head. "I do not seek revenge, only justice," he said. "Go to Prince Ferdinand and bring him here!"

Ariel's eyes darkened into doubt. "Will it be as thou promised, master? When thy plan is done, shall I be free?"

"Free as the wind, my Ariel," said Prospero. "I will break my spells, and no magic will ever hold you again."

Ariel glowed brightly, and flew off faster than Prospero's eyes could follow.

* * *

Prince Ferdinand was seated cross-legged on the sand. Salt water and the sun had bleached his brown hair almost blond, and his handsome face was lined with sadness.

Whenever he closed his eyes, he saw the massive waves that had swallowed the ship and cast him up on this uncharted island. He might never be found, and he wondered if it would be better to swim out to sea and join his drowned father than face a life of miserable loneliness...

His thoughts were suddenly interrupted
by lights dancing in front of his face,
swarming like bees.

They were so fascinating that Ferdinand could do nothing but stare at them. Then he heard music, and the singing of a sweet, high voice.

"Forget thy father, deep he lies,
With shining pearls set in his eyes.
Come with me now, Prince Ferdinand
And walk along the yellow sand!"

Ferdinand seemed to be caught up in a dream. Without a word he stood, and followed where the lights led him.

Prospero saw Ferdinand from afar, following bewitched behind Ariel's glimmering lights. When the young Prince was close by, Prospero touched Miranda on the shoulder, releasing her from the spell. Instantly, she woke, and the first thing she saw was Ferdinand. "Is this a spirit, Father?" she gasped.

"No, my child.
It is a man of
flesh and blood
like you and
me," Prospero
told her.

"But I thought all
men had white hair and
beards, like yours!" Miranda exclaimed.

Prospero smiled, and signalled to Ariel.
The dancing lights vanished,
and Ferdinand's trance
was broken. He saw
Miranda, and his eyes
filled with wonder at
her beauty. "Am
I still dreaming?"
he whispered.
"Is this a vision?"

"I am no vision, sir," Miranda said. "I am as real as you are...if you are indeed real." Shyly, she reached out her hand. Ferdinand reached out his, and their fingertips touched.

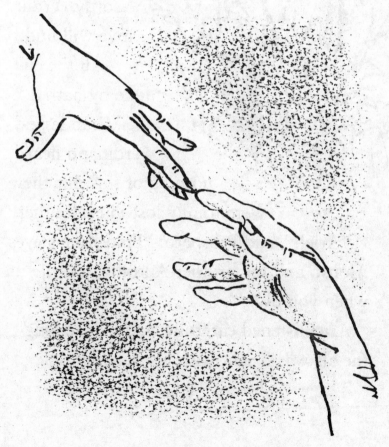

"I saw in the stars that you were meant for each other," Prospero said softly. "Your love will undo all the evil done by hatred." Miranda and Ferdinand heard nothing of this, for they were totally lost in each other.

"Ariel!" said Prospero. "Find King Alonso and my brother Antonio, and when you do..."

Ariel listened carefully, and before long the air was bright with his laughter.

On another part of the beach, two sailors
swayed across the sand, leaning against
each other to stop themselves
from falling over. One was Trinculo, a
thin man with ginger hair and a freckled
face, and his companion was Stephano,
who had a shock of grey hair and a
stomach as round as a watermelon.

They had been washed ashore together
with a cask of wine, which they had fast
consumed. Now they were so drunk, that
when Caliban jumped out from behind a
rock and grovelled at their feet, they were
not entirely sure that he was really there.

Caliban had been watching Trinculo and
Stephano for some time, and his quick,
cunning mind had seen a way to use them
to get rid of his master, Prospero.

"Gentle Gods!" Caliban cried. "Have
you come from the sky to save me?"

"He thinks we're Gods!" Trinculo giggled.

"Hmm, he's an ugly brute, but he knows good breeding when he sees it!" whispered

Stephano. "That's right, we're Gods from the moon," he said to Caliban.

"Save me!" Caliban begged. "Save me

from the wicked enchanter who has enslaved me, and I will give you all his treasure and be your faithful servant forever!"

"Enchanter?" yelped Trinculo, turning pale.

"Courage, Trinculo!" Stephano murmured. "And what kind of treasure might that be, good monster?"

"Gold," said Caliban. "And silver. And many jewels."

Stephano drew his cutlass and waved it so clumsily that he almost cut off his right ear. "Pirates, enchanters – it's all the same to me!" he boasted. "Take me to the villain! I'll carve him into thin slices!"

With a whoop of delight, Caliban led
the way along the jungle track to
Prospero's cave.

After the long walk through the
jungle's heat, and shadows, and strange
sounds, Stephano's head began to clear
and he no longer felt as bold as he had
earlier, and Trinculo was trembling like a
mouse's whiskers.

"Er, is it much further?" Stephano asked Caliban.

"There!" Caliban replied, pointing.

Trinculo stood on tiptoes and peered. He could see the mouth of a cave, filled with an ominous darkness.

"Why d-don't we walk s-side by s-side?" he jibbered. "Then n-nothing can harm us!"

Even as he spoke, the darkness in the cave began to move. It poured out of the cave-mouth, coiling like black mist – and the mist transformed itself into a pack of savage black dogs, with red eyes and

slavering fangs. Snapping and snarling,
the dogs bounded towards the intruders.

Trinculo and Stephano turned and ran
screaming into the jungle, with Caliban
close behind.

* * *

King Alonso and Antonio had also been wandering through the jungle for hours, and now they were desperate with thirst and hunger. Their fine clothes, ripped by cruel thorns, hung round them in tatters, and sweat streamed down their faces. Alonso, certain that Ferdinand was dead, was stricken with grief, and at last he slumped on to the trunk of a fallen tree.

"I can go no further!" he groaned. "I will wait here for death to put an end to my misery!"

Antonio glanced around uneasily. The jungle was an eerie place, full of shadows and whispering voices. "Just a little further, my lord!" he said. "I see a clearing not far ahead. Perhaps we will find a spring of fresh water there." The thought of water urged Alonso to his feet and together the two men stumbled towards the edge of the clearing.

Like a mirage, in the middle of the clearing stood a long table, piled with food and drink – golden platters of carved meats, whole roasted fowl, baskets of bread and golden jugs of wine.

Alonso and Antonio hurried towards it,
but before they could reach the feast, there
was a dazzling flash of light and Ariel
appeared. He hovered over the table in the
shape of a harpy – a monster with a human

head and the body of a gigantic eagle.
Alonso tried to snatch a jug of wine, but
the harpy hissed and slashed at him with its
bronze talons.

"Foul spirit, why do you torment us?"
Antonio sobbed.

"For thy betrayal of thy brother
Prospero and niece Miranda!" the harpy
screeched. "Thou and King Alonso did set
them in a boat and leave them to the
mercy of the ocean. Prepare thee for thy
punishment!"

Alonso and Antonio stared in amazement, wondering how the spirit had discovered their guilty secret. They expected the harpy to tear them into pieces, but instead it faded into a cloud of tiny lights that swirled like specks of dust floating in a beam of sunlight. The two men felt themselves fall into a waking sleep, and heard a voice speaking to them out of the cloud. "Come!" it said. "Follow, follow!"

***

From all over the island, the crew of the
wrecked ship came to gather on the beach
near Prospero's cave, drawn there by
magic – even Trinculo and Stephano, who
had aching heads and torn clothes from

where the hounds had snapped at them.
The sailors rejoiced to see friends they
thought had perished, and gazed about in
wonder. Had the storm only been a
dream, or were they dreaming now?

For there was their ship, undamaged, anchored close to the shore. The sailors laughed, and scratched their heads, unable to believe their luck.

Ariel brought Alonso and Antonio to the mouth of Prospero's cave, and broke their trance. Alonso gasped as Ferdinand and Miranda stepped out of the darkness, hand in hand, and his eyes blurred with tears. "What wonderful new world is this that has such people in it?" he wondered.

"The world that will be made when we return to Naples and our children are joined in marriage," said a voice.

Alonso and Antonio turned, and saw Prospero standing behind them. Antonio could not meet his brother's eyes, and hung his head in shame.

"Let our old hate be ended by their young love, Alonso," Prospero said. He came forward, and placed his hand on Antonio's shoulder. "I forgive you, brother," he said. "We will rule Milan together and end our days in peace. Now, go down to the shore and make ready to leave this island forever."

"Are you coming, Father?" asked
Miranda.

"In a moment, my child," Prospero
said. He waited until he was alone, then
whispered, "Ariel?"

Ariel grew out of emptiness. Too excited to hold one shape, he turned into a humming bird,

then a butterfly,

then a winged unicorn.

"I have burned my books of magic and my wizard's staff," Prospero declared. "You are free to go, my Ariel, but I shall sadly miss you!"

"And I shall miss thee, dear master!" said Ariel. "But look for me in springtime blossom, or when the summer breeze stirs thy curtain, or when the winter stars blaze bright. Until then, farewell!"

"Farewell, sweet spirit!" said Prospero, and he turned away so that Ariel would not see the tears in his eyes.

As the ship's sails unfurled and it began to glide away, Caliban came out of his hiding place in the jungle. He danced on the beach, turning cartwheels as he whooped, "I am King of the island! King!"

His voice frightened a flock of parrots who clattered out of the treetops and flew over Caliban in a great circle, their plumage glittering like the jewels in a royal crown.

Our revels now are ended. These our actors,
As I foretold you, were all spirits, and
Are melted into air, into thin air;

Prospero; IV.i.

Power in The Tempest

When we first meet Prospero, using magic to raise a storm and wreck a ship, he seems to be an evil magician. Prospero has enslaved the spirit, Ariel, and is now master to the monster Caliban. He has the power of magic at his fingertips, and is in a position of power over the island.

Gradually we learn that Prospero is not as wicked as he appears. He was once Duke of Milan, but was overthrown by his brother, Antonio, and Alonso, the King of Naples. Prospero and his little daughter, Miranda, were cast adrift in an open boat that brought them to the island. The ship that Prospero wrecks at the start of the play carries Antonio, his son Ferdinand, and King Alonso. They and all the sailors are washed safely ashore.

Prospero knows that Ferdinand and Miranda are destined to love each other, and that their love will put right the great wrong that was done to him twelve years before. He does not seek revenge, but justice, and when it finally comes, Prospero uses his power wisely and mercifully. Old enemies are humbled, but not humiliated. Prospero sets Ariel free and leaves Caliban master of the island once more.

The Tempest is one of Shakespeare's last plays, and he died two years after writing it. Many people believe that in the scene where Prospero destroys his magician's staff and books of magic, he speaks for Shakespeare, who is saying goodbye to the magical world of the theatre.

Hamlet

Cast List

The ghost of Hamlet's father

Hamlet
Son to the former King
Nephew to Claudius

Gertrude
Queen of Denmark
Mother to Hamlet

Horatio
Friend to Hamlet

Claudius
King of Denmark

Laertes

Son to Polonius

Ophelia

Daughter to Polonius

Polonius

Lord Chamberlain

A troop of travelling players

The Scene

Denmark in the thirteenth century.

Murder most foul, as in the best it is,
But this most foul, strange, and unnatural.

Ghost of Hamlet's father; I.v.

Hamlet

Snowflakes twirled in the wind that moaned around the battlements. I turned up the collar of my cloak against the cold, and kept my eyes fixed on the place where the guards had told me they had seen my father's ghost.

Horatio, my oldest friend, was with me. It was Horatio who had brought me the news that my father, the king, was dead – bitten by a snake while he was sleeping in the orchard – and it was Horatio who had stood by my side at my father's funeral. Something in me died too that day, and was sealed up in the Royal Tomb with my father. My grief was so great that it sucked the light and joy out of everything.

From the
courtyard below
came the sound of
drunken laughter.

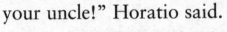

"Someone is
still celebrating
the marriage of
your mother and
your uncle!" Horatio said.

He meant it as a joke, but the joke
raised more black thoughts in my mind.

"How could she marry so soon after the
funeral?" I said. "How could she forget
my father so quickly?"

"You should be happy for her, my lord
Hamlet," said Horatio. "She has found
new happiness in the midst of sorrow, and
your uncle, Claudius, will rule Denmark
wisely until you come of age."

I laughed bitterly. I had seen cunning in Claudius's face, but no wisdom. I was about to say so, when midnight began to ring out from the turret above our heads.

And as the last stroke throbbed through the air, the darkness and the falling snow shaped themselves into the spirit of my father, beckoning to me.

Horatio gasped out a warning, but I paid no attention. I ran through the dancing flakes, my heart beating so fast that I thought it would burst. The ghost was dressed in armour, a circlet of gold gleaming against the black iron of its helm. Its face was my father's face, but twisted in agony, its eyes burning like cold, blue flames. Its voice was a groan of despair that sent shudders down my backbone.

133

"Hamlet, my son! My spirit cannot find rest until my murder has been avenged."

"Murder?" I cried.

"The serpent who stung me in the orchard was my brother, Claudius," said the ghost. "As I lay asleep, it was he who crept to my side and poured poison in my ear. Claudius took my life, my throne and now my wife. Avenge me, Hamlet!"

Before I could say more, the ghost faded into snowy blackness, and the echoes of its voice became the whistling of the wind.

My mind reeled. Had I really spoken to the ghost of my father, or was it a devil from Hell, sent to trick me into doing evil? I had suspected that Claudius might have had something to do with my father's death, but could I trust the word of a vision from beyond the grave? How could I be sure of the truth? How could I, the Prince of Denmark, not yet twenty years' old, avenge the death of a king?

I turned, and stumbled back to Horatio. His face was grey and he quivered with fear. "Such sights are enough to drive a man mad!" he whispered.

I laughed then, long and hard, because Horatio had unwittingly provided me with an answer.

Who could have more freedom than a mad prince? If I pretended to be mad, I could say whatever I wished and search for the truth without arousing Claudius's suspicion.

And so my plan took shape. I wore nothing but black. I wandered through the castle, weeping and sighing, seeking out shadowy places to brood. If anyone spoke to me, I answered with the first wild nonsense that came into my head, and all the time I watched Claudius, looking for the slightest sign of guilt. I cut myself off from all friends – except Horatio; I told him everything, for I knew he was the only one I could trust.

A rumour began to spread through the castle that grief had turned my wits. So far, my plan was a success, but it is one thing to invent a plan, and another thing to carry it through. The strain of pretending, of cutting myself off from kindness and good company, was almost too great to bear. There were times when I thought I truly had gone mad, when I felt I could no longer carry the burden of what the ghost had told me. If I avenged my father, my mother's new husband would be revealed as a murderer, and her happiness would be shattered; if I did not, my father's soul was doomed to eternal torment.

Worst of all, I was tortured by doubt. What if Claudius were innocent? What if I had been deceived by an evil spirit? Questions went spinning through my mind, like the stars spinning around the Earth.

Then one day, on a bleak afternoon, alone in my room, I drew my dagger and stared at it. The blade was sharp: if I used it on myself, death would come quickly, and all my doubts and worries would be over – but what then? Would I be sending my soul into an even worse torture?

I weighed the dagger in my hand, balancing the fear of what I must do to avenge my father against the fear of what might follow death. It seemed I lacked both the courage to go on with my life, and the courage to end it.

Hearing a knock at my door, I sheathed the dagger and called out, "Come in!" almost relieved at the interruption.

A woman entered. It was Lady Ophelia, her fair hair shining like a candle-flame, her eyes filled with love and concern.

My heart lifted, then sank. Ophelia and I had loved each other since we were children. Before my father's death, I had been certain that she was the one I would marry – but now everything had changed. There was no room in my heart for love.

"Lord Hamlet?" Ophelia said. "My father asks if you will attend the performance of the Royal Players tonight?"

As soon as she mentioned her father, I knew what was happening. Her father was Polonius, the Royal Chamberlain, a meddling fool who loved gossip and secrets. He had sent Ophelia to try and discover why I was acting so strangely. Ophelia would report everything I said to Polonius, and he would report it to Claudius. I was sickened: the castle of Elsinore was a place where brothers murdered brothers, wives forgot their husbands, and fathers used their daughters as spies.

I laughed carelessly, to hide the ache I felt when I looked at Ophelia's beautiful face. "Tell Lord Polonius that I shall be at the play," I said.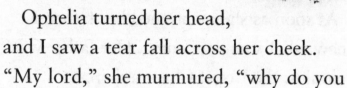

Ophelia turned her head, and I saw a tear fall across her cheek. "My lord," she murmured, "why do you never look at me the way you used to? There was a time when I believed you loved me, and wished us to marry, but now you seem so cold..."

I longed to tell her how much I loved her, and that my coldness was nothing more than acting, but I did not dare. "*You*, marry me?" I said roughly. "Marry no one, Ophelia! Wives and husbands are all cheats and liars. It would be better for you to join a convent and become a nun!"

At this she ran from the room, her sobs echoing through the corridor, making my heart break.

And then, just as I thought there was no end to my despair, an idea came – first a glimmer, then a gleam, then a burst of light brighter than the sun.

I hurried from my room and went to the Great Hall, where the actors were setting up their stage. I found their leader, a tall man with a look of my uncle about him. After chatting for a few moments, I said casually, "Do you know the play *The Murder of Gonzago*?" "Certainly, my lord!" came the reply.

I handed the man a purse filled with gold. "Act it tonight," I said. "But I want you to make some changes to the story. Listen carefully..."

I meant to turn the play from an entertainment into a trap – a trap to catch a King.

* * *

That evening, while the audience watched the stage, I watched Claudius. At first he showed little interest in the story, preferring to whisper to my mother and kiss her fingers in a way that filled me with loathing – but gradually the skill of the players won his attention.

At the end of the first scene, exactly according to my instructions, the actor playing Duke Gonzago lay down as though asleep and his nephew Lucianus – played by the actor who resembled Claudius – crept up on him and poured poison into his ear.

Even though the light in the hall was dim, I could see the deathly pallor of Claudius's face as he watched this scene. His eyes grew troubled, and he raised a trembling hand towards the stage.

I knew then that I was gazing at the face of a murderer, and that everything the ghost had told me was true.

"No!" Claudius cried out, springing to his feet. "Lights! Bring more lights!"

But all the torches in the world would not light the darkness in his mind. His nerve failed and he hurried from the hall.

Mother made to follow him, but I stopped her at the door. "Do not delay me. I must go to the King!" she said. "Something is wrong."

"And I know what," I told her. "I must talk to you. I will come to your room in an hour. Make sure you are alone, and tell no one of our meeting."

✳ ✳ ✳

But I underestimated Claudius's cunning, and the power he had over my mother. When she let me into her room, there was a coldness in her expression and I guessed that she had been speaking to my uncle. Before I could say a word, she said, "Hamlet, you have deeply offended your royal stepfather."

"And you have offended my dead father," I replied.

Mother frowned at me, puzzled. "What do you mean?" she demanded.

"You offended him the day you abandoned your mourning robes in exchange for a wedding gown," I said. "The day you married a liar and a murderer!"

"I won't listen!" Mother shouted. She began to cover her ears with her hands and I caught hold of her wrists to prevent her – she had to hear the truth. Mother screamed in alarm, and then I heard a voice from behind the drawn curtains at her window, calling out, "Help! Murder!"

I was certain it was Claudius – who else would skulk and spy in my mother's bedroom? I drew my sword and plunged it into the curtain, filled with fierce joy that my father was avenged at last...

But it was the body of Lord Polonius that tumbled into the room; I had killed an innocent man.

"You meddling old fool!" I groaned. "What were you doing there?"

"Following my orders," said a voice. I turned and saw Claudius in the doorway, with two armed guards. A triumphant light glinted in his eyes. "I was afraid you might harm your mother if you were alone with her," Claudius went on.

"Your madness has made you violent, Hamlet. You must leave Denmark tonight. I shall send you to friends in England, who will care for you until you are back in your right mind. Guards, take the Prince away!"

Neither my mother nor the guards saw the mocking smile that flickered on his lips, but as soon as I saw it, I knew that Claudius intended me never to return from England. I would be imprisoned, and then secretly murdered.

While I had been trying to trap my uncle, he had been setting a trap for me, and now it had snapped shut.

They bundled me into a windowless
carriage and locked the doors and I
was driven speedily through the night.

I could see nothing, and could hear only
the rattling of the wheels and the cracking
of the driver's whip, keeping the horses at
full gallop.

After several hours, the carriage arrived at a port, and I was placed on a ship that set sail almost as soon as I was aboard. I made no attempt to escape. It was all over: my father was unavenged, Claudius had outwitted me, and I was as good as dead.

Just before
dawn broke,
my life seemed
to become some
strange dream,
for the most
unlikely thing
happened: I
was rescued by
Danish pirates.
They captured the
ship and murdered
most of the crew,
but when they discovered
who I was, panic seized them.
Fearing that they would be hunted down
by the Danish fleet, the pirates sailed back
to Denmark and put me ashore at a little
fishing village.

There I found lodgings and wrote letters to Horatio, and to my mother. I told her that I would return to Elsinore and right all the wrongs that had been done – though I did not tell her what those wrongs were.

The next day, I bought a horse and set off, certain that Fate had returned me to Denmark to complete my revenge. There was no more doubt in my mind – Claudius was guilty, and I would make him answer for his crime.

I was still some way from the castle when I was met by Horatio, who had ridden out to find me. There was a darkness in my friend's face, and I knew he was the bearer of ill tidings.

"My lord," he said, "the Lady Ophelia is dead. Claudius told her that you had killed her father, and the grief drove her so mad that she drowned herself."

Tears blurred my sight. What had I done to my beloved Ophelia! In another time and place, our love might have grown into happiness...

"Ophelia's brother, Laertes, has sworn to kill you for the deaths of his father and sister," Horatio went on, "but Claudius persuaded Laertes to settle his differences with you in a fencing match, in front of the whole court. I have seen the King whispering to Laertes in private, and I am sure they are plotting against you. Turn back, my lord! Escape while you can to somewhere you will be safe!"

"No, I must go to Elsinore," I told him. "My destiny awaits me there. We cannot escape our destinies, Horatio, we can only be ready for them, and I am ready."

And so the ghost, Claudius, the pirates and my destiny have brought me back, to the torch-light and candles of the Great Hall at Elsinore. Courtiers and nobles chatter idly and make wagers on the outcome of the

duel. There, on the royal thrones, sit my uncle and my mother. She smiles at me and looks proud; he is anxious, and keeps glancing slyly at Laertes. Laertes is filled with a cold hatred that makes his eyes shine like moonlight on ice.

Horatio takes
my cloak and
hands me a
rapier. His face is
pale and worried.
He leans close and
whispers, "Have a
care, my lord! There
is death in Laertes' look."

I smile: death is everywhere in the castle

of Elsinore tonight,
and I can feel my
father's spirit
hovering over me.
Claudius raises
his right arm.
"Let the contest
begin!" he
commands.

The blades of our rapiers snick and squeal. Our shadows, made huge and menacing by the torches, flicker on the walls as we duck and dodge. Laertes is a skilled swordsman, but rage and hate have made him clumsy. He drops his guard to strike at me, I flick my wrist, and the point of my rapier catches his arm.

One of the marshals shouts, "A hit! First hit to Prince Hamlet!"

Laertes bows, his forehead slick with sweat. "Let us take a cup of wine and catch our breath, my lord," he says.

The wine cups are on a table near the thrones. Laertes and I step towards them, and my mother suddenly snatches up one of the cups. "A toast, to honour my beloved son!" she announces.

"No!" hisses Claudius. He reaches out as if to dash the cup from my mother's lips, but he is too late: she has drunk the wine down to the dregs.

There is just time for me to see a look of horror on Claudius's face, and then, without warning, Laertes wheels around and slashes at me with his sword. I parry the blow, realising that this is no longer a contest – I am fighting for my life.

I see Laertes'
eyes, blind with
fury. I watch his
mouth twist
itself into an
ugly snarl. He
clutches at me
and tries to
stab under my
arm, but I
catch the sword
in my left hand
and I wrench it from
his grasp. A pain like fire
burns against my palm,
and my fingers are wet with blood.

I step back, throw Laertes my rapier
and take his in my right hand. *En
garde!* I say.

We fight on, but something is wrong. Laertes looks terrified, and his breath comes in sobs. The pain in my hand is fierce, throbbing up into my forearm – I have suffered from sword-cuts before, but none as painful as this.

Laertes lunges desperately at me, and the point of my sword scratches through his shirt; a spurt of red stains the whiteness of the linen.

Laertes reels back. "We are dead men!" he groans. "The King spread poison on the blade – the same poison that he poured into your wine cup!"

I see all now. I understand the hot agony that is creeping through my left arm and across my chest.

Laertes cries out, "The King is a
murderer!" and crumples to the floor.
At the same time, my mother screams and
topples from her throne.

There is no time left. I must act quickly, before the pain reaches my heart. I stagger towards Claudius and he cringes in his throne, covering his face with his hands.

"Traitor!" I say, and drive the poisoned sword deep into his heart.

Voices shout...people are running. I fall back, and someone catches me. I think it is Horatio, but I cannot see him clearly, for a darkness is falling before my eyes...coming down like the snow falling, that night on the battlements...

Through the darkness, I seem to see
a light...and my father's face...and
everything drops away behind me...

Horatio's voice whispers, "Farewell,
sweet Prince!"

And the rest is silence.

There's a divinity that shapes our ends,
Rough-hew them how we will.

Hamlet; V.ii.

Revenge in Hamlet

In *Hamlet*, Shakespeare portrays a young man who has been educated to be a thinker, but who becomes a man of action, motivated by the dark force of revenge.

When Hamlet discovers from his father's ghost that the old king's death was not an accident but murder, he is torn in two. The ghost claims that the murderer is Claudius, his own brother, who has recently married Hamlet's mother. Is the ghost telling the truth, or is it a demon sent from hell to tempt the prince into an evil act? Hamlet is left confused and constantly tortured by doubt. He can't decide what to do.

In a desperate attempt to uncover the truth, Hamlet pretends to be mad. He kills Polonius by mistake, and this leads to the accidental death of

Ophelia, with whom Hamlet was once in love.

In a thrilling climax, Hamlet agrees to a fencing match with Laertes. Laertes, having lost his father and sister, is full of despair and desire for his own revenge. He fights with a poisoned sword given to him by Claudius, who suspects that Hamlet knows too much.

In Elizabethan times, this final scene of *Hamlet* would have been full of spectacularly gory visual effects. To make sword-fights seem more realistic, pigs' bladders filled with blood were hidden in the actors' costumes, and pierced with the point of a sword or dagger.

The audience would have been spellbound by the dark tale of revenge, where a prince succeeds in avenging his father's death – but at a terrible cost.

Henry V

Cast List

King Henry V

Duke of Exeter
Uncle to the King

Earl of Cambridge
A conspirator against the King

Michael Williams
A soldier in the King's army

A French ambassador

A French messenger

The Scene
England and France in the fifteenth century.

I see you stand like greyhounds in the slips,
Straining upon the start. The game's afoot.
Follow your spirit, and upon this charge
Cry, 'God for Harry! England and Saint George!'

King Henry; III.i.

Henry V

Hardly anyone called the new King
'Henry'. When they talked about him they
said 'Hal' or 'Harry', or used one of his
other nicknames. Everyone knew what a
wild and rebellious teenager the young
prince had been.

Harry had spent more time with rascally old Sir John Falstaff, learning how to drink and gamble than he had with his royal father. Now the reckless young Harry was King, but no one knew what sort of king he would be. Some thought he would be a disaster, others said that only time would tell, but all were aware that the young King faced a difficult time as the new English monarch.

England and France had been at war for twenty-five years, and though the two countries had agreed a truce, the truce was an uneasy one. A weak English king who didn't have the support of his people might give the French just the chance they wanted to carry out a successful invasion...

* * *

One morning, not long after Henry's coronation, the nobles of the High Council were gathered together in the Reception Chamber of the King's palace in London. Among them was the Duke of Exeter, the King's uncle. He knew that Henry was now about to face his most challenging test. 'How young and lonely he looks on that great throne,' Exeter thought. 'He has his mother's dark hair and soft eyes – but does he have any of his father's courage, I wonder?'

His question was soon answered, for just then the doors of the great chamber opened and an ambassador from the Dauphin, the Crown Prince of France, entered. The ambassador was a perfumed dandy with his curled beard, and the clothes he wore were as brightly-coloured as a peacock's feathers. Behind him, two guards carried a large wooden chest which they set down on the floor.

The ambassador gave an elaborate bow. "Your Highness," he said, in a voice as smooth as honey. "My master, the Dauphin, sends greetings."

"I want more than greetings," Henry replied coldly. "I asked King Charles to give me back the French lands that my father won from him. What is his answer?"

The ambassador ran his fingers through the curls of his beard and smirked. "The King is busy with important matters," he said. "His Majesty thought that since the Dauphin is closer to you in age, it would be better for him to deal with your request."

Henry felt a sting of anger at the ambassador's insolent tone, but he kept his voice calm. "And what is the Dauphin's message?" he asked.

"The Dauphin thinks you are a little too young to bother yourself with affairs of state," said the ambassador, gesturing towards the wooden chest. "So he has sent a present which he thinks will be more suitable than the right to French dukedoms."

The ambassador clicked his fingers
and the guards opened the lid of the
chest. It was filled with tennis balls. One
of them fell out and rolled to the foot of
Henry's throne.

The nobles glanced at each other anxiously. King Henry had been insulted and humiliated in front of all his courtiers. How would he respond?

Henry leaned over and picked up the ball at his feet. He bounced it once, and caught it in his right hand. "Tell the Dauphin that he has begun a game with me that he'll wish he had never started,"  he said. "His mockery will turn these tennis balls into cannon balls! The people of France may be laughing at the Dauphin's joke, but they'll weep before I'm finished!"

The ambassador's face went deathly pale. He bowed low and left the chamber. When the door closed behind him, the nobles began to talk among themselves.  Most of them glanced admiringly at Henry, but the Earl of Cambridge scowled at the King. He raised his voice above the hubbub in the chamber and said, "Your Majesty spoke hastily. You should have sought the advice of older and wiser men before plunging our country into war."

"An insult to me is an insult to the English people!" Henry snapped. "And besides, my lord Cambridge, I don't listen to the advice of traitors!"

Cambridge started as though someone had jabbed him with a knife point and his eyes bulged with fear.

"You thought that because of my youth, I could easily be deceived," Henry went on, "but I've found you out. You betrayed your country for French gold and worked as a spy for King Charles. Guards, take him to the Tower!"

The nobles stared in astonishment at the disclosure of Cambridge's treachery and at seeing the determination of their young King. He was wiser and stronger-minded than any of them had realised.

Men from all over the country answered the young King's call to war with France.

Blacksmiths,

farm-workers,

wheelwrights,
weavers and clerks...

...all left their homes and marched along
the roads that led to Southampton.

The younger men thought that war would be a kind of holiday and were eager for fame and glory; others, who had fought before and knew what battle was like, were grim-faced and silent.

At Southampton, the men began their training. Hour after hour and day after day they marched and drilled. At the archery butts men with longbows practised until their aim was true.

Slowly, the raggle-taggle band of volunteers was transformed into an army. When all was ready, the English battle fleet set sail for the French port of Harfleur.

* * *

It took all day for Henry's men to cross the Channel and unload the ships. The men spent the night on the beach and were woken in the grey hours before

dawn to sharpen their weapons and make
ready their siege-ladders and battering-
rams. On the skyline the walls of Harfleur
looked like an ominous cloud.

When the sun rose, Henry rode out in front of his men on his dapple-grey war-horse, the early morning light glinting on his armour. "The English are a peaceful nation," he told the troops, "but when war comes, we can fight like tigers! Let the light of battle blaze in your eyes, to burn the courage of your enemies! Let your cry be: *God for Harry, England and St George!*"

Cannons roared like a gigantic wave
breaking on the shore as the English army
charged. By nightfall, Harfleur had fallen.

Henry was planning to advance to the port of Calais, which was already in English possession. The next morning a messenger arrived from King Charles.

"The King commands that you surrender to him and leave France while you still can!" the messenger declared scornfully. "He is camped at Agincourt with an army of fifty thousand. If you do not agree to his terms, he will advance and crush you!"

"Your Majesty!" the Duke of Exeter murmured. "We only have four thousand men. If the French attack us here, all will be lost!"

"Then we must go to them, Uncle," Henry said calmly. He turned to the messenger. "Tell King Charles that his army is in my way," he said. "I will march to Agincourt and, if he does not step aside, the earth will be red with French blood!"

And so the English advanced to Agincourt and set up camp facing the French, on a plain between two woods. When the French saw the size of the English army they whistled and jeered, beating their swords against their shields to make a great clamour.

But Henry shut his
ears to their taunts
and concentrated
on positioning
his forces. He
discussed battle
plans with his
commanders late into
the night and after they had left his tent,
Henry tried to rest, but a whirlpool of
doubts and fears swirled
in his mind, and he
could not sleep.
Hoping to calm
himself, he put
on a hooded
cloak and went
walking through
the camp.

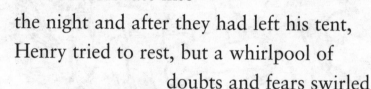

Men lay asleep, huddled around fires. The air was filled with the sound of snores, or voices shouting out in terror through nightmares. Across the plain glimmered the fires of the French camp, as numberless as the stars on a winter's night.

Henry was so deep in thought that he didn't notice a sentry on guard beside one camp fire until he almost walked on to the point of the man's spear.

"Who goes there?" barked the sentry.

"A friend," Henry replied.

"Who is your commander?"

"The Duke of Exeter."

The guard lowered his spear and pulled a face. "A fine soldier!" he grunted. "If he were leading the army instead of the King, we wouldn't be in this mess. I bet young Harry wishes he was back in London, tucked up safe in bed."

"The King wishes himself nowhere but here," said Henry.

The guard turned his head to spit into the fire. Light from the flames played across his broken nose and the long scar on his left cheek.

"Kings!" he growled. "They do the arguing, but it's the likes of you and me who do the fighting and the dying!"

"Tomorrow the King will fight in the front line, alongside his men, you will see," said Henry.

"I'll wager a week's wages that he'll be at the back, with a fast horse ready for his escape!" the guard said bitterly.

"Very well," said Henry. "If we both survive, find me when the battle's over and we'll see who was right. What's your name?"

"Michael Williams," said the guard. "What's yours?"

"Harry le Roy," Henry said with a smile, then he passed on and disappeared into the darkness.

* * *

In the early hours of the morning a thunderstorm broke. Rain fell mercilessly, drenching English and French alike and turning the plain into a sea of mud. The rain stopped just before dawn, but the sky was still filled with heavy black clouds.

The first line
of the French
army took
the field, led
by knights on
horseback.
The plumes
on their helmets
fluttered brightly
against the dark sky, and their armour
shone like silver. Behind them
ran infantrymen in chain-mail
coats, carrying blue
shields painted with
golden fleurs-de-lis.

Henry ordered his
archers to stand
ready and wait for
his signal.

The French knights broke into a gallop. The hooves of the horses shook the ground, and spattered their riders with mud. The knights lowered their lances and screamed out a battle cry, but halfway to the English line, the French

horses ran into boggy ground and the charge faltered. The knights pulled at their reins in panic, turning their horses to try and find firmer footing. The infantrymen caught up, and all was a surging chaos of whinnying horses and cursing men.

Henry drew his sword and swept it high above his head. "Fire!" he bellowed.

At his command, a thousand arrows left a thousand longbows and made a sound like the wind sighing through the boughs of a forest. A deadly hail struck the French, piercing armour, and flesh, and bone. Knights fell from their saddles and startled horses bolted, trampling anyone who stood in their way.

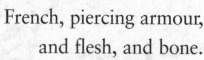

Volley after volley of arrows whistled down, until the only movement on the battlefield came from the wounded as they attempted to crawl back to safety.

A second line of French troops charged.
Once more the English archers stopped
them. The French tried to retreat, but ran

into their own third line as it came up
behind them. It was then that Henry led
his men in a charge. The two armies met
with a clash like a clap of thunder.

The fighting lasted for two hours. The French soldiers, dismayed and confused, found that their commanders had been killed and there was no one to give them orders. They fought

bravely, but the fury of the English attack proved too much for them, and at last they broke ranks and fled.

Seven thousand Frenchmen died at Agincourt, including many great noblemen. The English lost only a hundred men.

* * *

That night, at sunset, a French messenger rode into the English camp carrying a white flag of truce. It was the same man who had come to Harfleur, but this time he was not haughty. His armour was dented and there was dirt and blood on his face.

"King Charles begs for peace," he said humbly. "He will return all the lands that you claim and he asks you to accept the hand of his daughter, Princess Catherine, so that your two families may be united in peace forever."

"Tell the King that I accept," said Henry. "We will meet, and draw up a peace treaty."

235

That night, there were celebrations in
the English camp and just before midnight,
Henry slipped away from his commanders
and went in search of Michael Williams.
He found him at the same guard point as
on the previous night.

When Williams saw Henry, he dropped to one knee. "Your Majesty," he mumbled. "I did not know who you were last night, but I recognised you today when you led the charge."

"So," said Henry, smiling. "I won the wager."

"I was a fool to speak the way I did last night!" said the sentry apologetically.

Henry put his hand on the man's
shoulder and took a bag of gold coins
from his belt. He handed it to the
astonished guard.

"Here," Henry said. "You spoke your
mind last night. I hope that honest men will
always speak to me as openly as you did."

✳ ✳ ✳

So King Henry the Fifth won a famous victory – and more importantly, he won the hearts of all his subjects. Now they respected him as a ruler, but they also loved him because he understood the lives of ordinary people, and was always ready to listen to them.

And he won more than his subjects' hearts, for when he met Catherine, the French princess, they fell in love at once – even though she could not speak English and his clumsy French made her laugh. With their marriage, the bitter war with France was ended in feasting and friendship.

This star of England. Fortune made his sword,
By which the world's best garden he achieved,

Chorus; V.ii.

Patriotism in Henry V

There were no newspapers, radio or television in Shakespeare's time, so it is difficult to know what ordinary people thought about what was happening in the world around them. However, dramatists often reflected popular opinions in their plays, and *Henry V* is an example of this.

Shakespeare wrote the play in 1599, the same year that the Earl of Essex led an army to put down a rising in Ireland. Many hoped that Essex would win as famous a victory as Henry V at Agincourt.

The play is based on historical events, but Shakespeare shapes the facts to present a picture of a country uniting under a strong leader to face a fearsome enemy. The rousing, patriotic speeches in the play capture the patriotic mood of

Elizabethan England.

In *Henry V*, no one expects Henry to be a good king because of his wild behaviour as a prince. But once on the throne, he displays wisdom and courage.

On the night before the battle of Agincourt, Henry, disguised as an ordinary foot soldier, has a conversation with a sentry. Shakespeare presents a leader who is not distant from his people. This is a king in touch with his subjects, and one who values their honesty.

In the battle that follows, huge numbers of the French army are killed, while only a few Englishmen lose their lives. The audience, cheering the actors at the end of the performance, would also have been expressing their patriotism and pride in their country and its achievements.

Shakespeare and the Globe Theatre

Some of Shakespeare's most famous plays were first performed at the Globe Theatre, which was built on the South Bank of the River Thames in 1599.

Going to the Globe was a different experience from going to the theatre today. The building was roughly circular in shape, but with flat sides: a little like a doughnut crossed with a fifty-pence piece. Because the Globe was an open-air theatre, plays were only put on during daylight hours in spring and summer. People paid a penny to stand in the central space and watch a play, and this part of the audience became known as 'the groundlings' because they stood on the ground. A place in the tiers of seating beneath the thatched roof, where there was a slightly better view and less chance of being rained on, cost extra.

The Elizabethans did not bath very often and the audiences at the Globe were smelly. Fine ladies and gentlemen in the more expensive seats sniffed perfume and bags of sweetly-scented herbs to cover the stink rising from the groundlings.

There were no actresses on the stage; all the female characters in Shakespeare's plays would have been acted by boys, wearing wigs and make-up. Audiences were not well-behaved. People clapped and cheered when their favourite actors came on stage; bad actors were jeered at and sometimes pelted with whatever came to hand.

Most Londoners worked hard to make a living and in their precious free time they liked to be entertained. Shakespeare understood the magic of the theatre so well that today, almost four hundred years after his death, his plays still cast a spell over the thousands of people that go to see them.

READ ON FOR AN
EXTRACT FROM

Macbeth

Cast List

The Three Witches – or Weird Sisters

Macbeth

Thane of Glamis
General to King Duncan

Lady Macbeth

Wife to Macbeth

Banquo

General to King Duncan

King Duncan

King of Scotland

Malcolm and Donalbain

The King's sons

Macduff

Thane of Fife

A servant of Glamis Castle

Two Murderers

The Scene

Scotland in the eleventh century.

Macbeth

All day, the three witches waited on the edge of the battlefield. Hidden by mist and magic, they watched the Scottish army win a victory over the invading forces of Norway, and after the fight was done they lingered on, gloating over the moans of the dying.

As thunder rolled overhead and rain lashed down, one of the witches raised her long, hooked nose to the wind and sniffed like a dog taking a scent. "He will be here soon," she said.

The second witch stroked the tuft of silvery hair that sprouted from her chin, and grinned, showing her gums. "I hear the sound of hooves, sisters," she said.

The third witch held up a piece of rock crystal in front of her milky, blind eyes. Inside the crystal, something seemed to move. "I see him!" she screeched. "He comes! Let the spell begin."

* * *

Two Scottish generals rode slowly away
from the battlefield, their heads lowered
against the driving rain.

One was Macbeth, the Thane of Glamis,
the bravest soldier in King Duncan's army.
He was tall, broad-shouldered and had a
warrior's face, broken-nosed and scarred
from old fights.

His companion and friend Banquo was younger and slimmer, with a mouth that was quick to smile, although he wasn't smiling now.

Macbeth's dark eyes were distant as he recalled the details of the day's slaughter. 'A hard fight to protect an old, feeble King,' he thought. 'If I ruled Scotland…' His mind drifted off into a familiar daydream: he saw himself seated on the throne, with the golden crown of Scotland circling his brow…

Read

MACBETH

and more Shakespeare classics in